John Fretwell

Newfoundland and the Jingoes

An Appeal to England's Honor

John Fretwell

Newfoundland and the Jingoes
An Appeal to England's Honor

ISBN/EAN: 9783337327422

Printed in Europe, USA, Canada, Australia, Japan

Cover: Foto ©Andreas Hilbeck / pixelio.de

More available books at **www.hansebooks.com**

NEWFOUNDLAND AND THE JINGOES

JINGOES

AN APPEAL TO ENGLAND'S HONOR

BY

JOHN FRETWELL

" To be taken into the American Union is to be adopted into a partnership. To belong as a Crown Colony to the British Empire, as things stand, is no partnership at all.

" It is to belong to a power which sacrifices, as it has always sacrificed, the interest of its dependencies to its own. The blood runs freely through every vein and artery of the American body corporate. Every single citizen feels his share in the life of his nation. Great Britain leaves her Colonies to take care of themselves, refuses what they ask, and forces on them what they had rather be without.

" If I were a West Indian, I should feel that under the stars and stripes I should be safer than I was at present from political experimenting. I should have a market in which to sell my produce where I should be treated as a friend. I should have a power behind me and protecting me, and I should have a future to which I could look forward with confidence. America would restore me to hope and life: Great Britain allows me to sink, contenting herself with advising me to be patient. Why should I continue loyal when my loyalty was so contemptuously valued ? "— JAMES ANTHONY FROUDE (from " The English in the West Indies," Nov. 15, 1887).

" In the United States is Canada's natural market for buying as well as for selling, the market which her productions are always struggling to enter through every opening in the tariff wall, for exclusion from which no distant market either in England or elsewhere can compensate her, the want of which brings on her commercial atrophy, and drives the flower of her youth by thousands and tens of thousands over the line.

" The Canadian North-west remains unpeopled while the neighboring States of the Union are peopled, because it is cut off from the continent to which it belongs by a fiscal and political line."— GOLDWIN SMITH, D.C.L., in " Questions of the Day," page 159 (Macmillan & Co., London, 1893).

PREFACE.

It would be evidence of gross ignorance, or something worse, to pretend that the United States, under like conditions, would have treated the Newfoundlanders better than England has done. It would be especially so after the humiliating spectacle presented to the world by our Democratic majorities last year in Congress and in the State and city of New York.

With material resources superior to those of any other country in the world, we are obliged to appeal to the European money-lender for gold.

Even the chosen head of our Tory Democracy tells Congress that we must sacrifice $16,000,000 to obtain gold on the terms offered by his Secretary of the Treasury.

England's past blunders have been singularly favorable to American interests, when real statesmen were at the helm in Washington. Any strategist can see that, if Lord Palmerston, instead of bullying weak Greece and China, had done justice to Newfoundland, his government might have acquired so strong a position in America as to seriously imperil the preservation of the Union some thirty years ago. That he failed to do his duty was as fortunate for the United States as it was unfortunate for Newfoundland. To-day, but for the emasculating influence of our Tory Democracy, England's blunders in the same island would be profitable to the United States.

Even for our small and expensive navy we cannot find sufficient able seamen among our citizens; and the starving fishermen of Newfoundland are just the men we need. But there is no money in the national treasury to pay them; while our ridiculous immigration and suffrage laws exclude the men we need, and enable the scum of Europe to influence our legislation.

I trust this tract may suggest to some Englishmen the best way to prevent a repetition of the present distress, and so show the world that, after all, loyalty is sometimes appreciated in imperial circles. The old project of a rapid line of steamers from Bay St. George to Chaleurs Bay, giving England communication via Newfoundland with Montreal in less than five days, has been revived; but the route is closed by winter ice, and too far north for the United States.

A better route, open all the year round, is that from Port aux Basques to Neil's Cove, a distance of only fifty-two miles by sea against two hundred and fifty miles from Bay St. George to Paspebiac or Shippegan; and still better is the route via Port aux Basques and Louisbourg, which will soon be connected with the American lines, with a single break of three miles at the Gut of Canso Ferry. With all its faults, British rule has one advantage over that of all other colonial powers: it gives the foreigner, no matter what his faith or nation, exactly the same commercial rights as the British subject; and so, although Newfoundland will lose by the exclusion of its fish from our protected markets, and by the diplomatic inability of the British government to protect it from the effects of French bounties and treaty rights, the enlightened selfishness of the New Englander will find that "there is money for him" in the development of those resources which have been so singularly neglected by the British capitalists who invest their money in the most rotten schemes that Yankee ingenuity can invent.

J. F.

FEB 11, 1895.

AUTHORITIES.

IN the following pages I have drawn largely on the well-known works of Hatton and Harvey, Bonnycastle, Pedley, Bishop Howley, and Spearman's article in the *Westminster Review* for 1892, concerning Newfoundland; and, on the general question, on Froude's "England to the Defeat of the Spanish Armada," Lecky's "History of England in the Eighteenth Century," Blaine's "Twenty Years of Congress," Hansard's Debates, "The Annual Register," McCarthy's "History of our own Times," and the Blue Books of the British government.

To the tourist who proposes to visit the island I can recommend Rev. Moses Harvey's "Newfoundland in 1894," published in St. John's, as the best guide to the island. Mr. Harvey has also written an excellent article on the island for Baedeker's "Canada." For the hunter, painter, photographer, angler, yachtsman, or geologist, there is not a more attractive excursion, for from one to three months, along the whole American coast than that through and round Newfoundland.

J. F.

NEWFOUNDLAND AND THE JINGOES.

BY JOHN FRETWELL.

THE most prominent and able intellectual representative of the money power in the world, the London *Times*, writes of Newfoundland : —

" Even if we were disposed to do so, we cannot in our position as a naval power view with indifference the disaster to, and possibly the ruin of, a colony we may sometimes regard as amongst the most valuable of our naval stations. Neither can we view the position without consideration for the wide-spread suffering that an absolute refusal to grant assistance would entail. It is probable that a cheaper system of administration would retrieve the position without casting an overwhelmingly heavy burden upon the imperial tax-payers. If we interpret public feeling aright, it will be in favor of giving the colony the help that may be found essential ; but, if the assistance required takes anything like the radical proportion that at present seems necessary, it can only be granted at a price,— the surrender of the Constitution and the return of Newfoundland to the condition of a crown colony."

While we may safely concede to the editors of the *Times* as much " consideration for wide-spread suffering " as to a Jay Gould or a Napoleon, the above-quoted words are significant, because they show that what the ruling powers in England would never concede to charity or justice they will give to self-interest, now that the *Times* has discovered " there is money in it."

But to us Americans the words have their lesson also. Newfoundland not only belongs to our Continental system,

but it can never be really prosperous until it becomes a
State in our Union. What it is to-day, New England might
have been, had it not been delivered by the Continental
forces, and by the French navy, from the rule of British
Tories. And, as a member of our Union, this island, five
times the size of Massachusetts, might not only be as prosperous as Rhode Island or Connecticut, but also the chief
training ground for our future navy, which, checked by the
piracies of the British-built "Alabama," will become in the
near future an indispensable necessity of our national existence.

Since the English people seem to have taken to heart, far
more than his own countrymen have done, the lesson taught
by our Captain Mahan in his "Influence of the Sea-power
in History," it is well that we should consider the past
history of England's relations to that first-born colony
which she has so infamously sacrificed, and for whose misfortunes she alone is responsible.

The lesson that we may learn from that history is quite
as much needed by the American as by the Briton. Ed-
mund R. Spearman, writing in the *Westminster Review* (Vol.
137, page 403, 1892), says : —

"No English Homer has yet risen to tell the tale of Newfoundland, shrouded in mystery and romance, the daring
invasion and vicissitudes of those exhaustless fisheries,
the battle of life in that seething cauldron of the North
Atlantic, where the swelling billows never rest, and the hur-
ricane only slumbers to bring forth the worse dangers of
the fog-bank and the iceberg. Fierce as has been during
the four centuries the fight for the fisheries by European
rivals, their petty racial quarrels sink into insignificance
before the general struggle for the harvest. The Atlantic
roar hides all minor pipings. The breed of fisher-folk from
these deep-sea voyagings consist of the toughest specimens
of human endurance. All other dangers which lure men to
venture everything for excitement or for fortune, the torrid

heat or arctic cold, the battle against man or beast, the desert or the jungle, all land adventures are as nothing compared to the daring of the hourly existence of the heroic souls whose lives are cast upon the banks of Newfoundland. The fishermen may seem wild and reckless, rough and illiterate; but supreme danger and superlative sacrifice breed noble qualities, and beneath the rough exterior of the fisherman you will never fail to find a MAN, and no cheap imitation of the genuine article. None but a man can face for a second time the frown of the North Atlantic, that exhibition of mighty, all-consuming power, beside the sober reality of which all the ecstasies of poets and painters are puny failures. Among these heroes of the sea England's children have always been foremost. We should expect England to be especially proud of such an offspring, familiar with their struggles, and ever heedful of their welfare, lending an ear to their claims or complaints above all others. Strange to say, it has always been the exact reverse."

Though discovered by John and Sebastian Cabot in 1494, "the twenty-fourth of June at five o'clock in the morning," it was not until ninety years later that the island was formally organized as an English colony (Aug. 5, 1582, by Sir Humphrey Gilbert).

The persecutions of Bloody Mary and the massacre of St. Bartholomew had roused the indignation of Englishmen to the highest pitch. They were ready for any risk in open war against France and Spain, but Queen Elizabeth was always trying to shirk responsibility; and so the sea-captains who would avenge the wrongs done to the Protestants were obliged to run the risk of being condemned as pirates.

One of them wrote to Queen Elizabeth, Nov. 6, 1577, offering to fit out ships, well armed, for the Banks of Newfoundland, where some twenty-five thousand fishermen went out from France, Spain, and Portugal every summer to catch the food of their Catholic fast days. He proposed to treat these fishermen as the Huguenots of France had been treated,— to bring away the best of their ships, and to burn the rest. Nine days after the date of this letter Francis Drake sailed from Plymouth, commanding a fleet of five ships, equipped by a company of private adventurers, of whom Queen Elizabeth was the largest shareholder. Fortunately, they never committed the horrible crime suggested in that letter. In those five ships, says Froude, lay the germ of Great Britain's ocean empire.

In 1585 Sir John Hawkins, who had meanwhile annexed Newfoundland to the English Dominion, proposed again to take a fleet to the Fishing Banks, whither half the sailors of Spain and Portugal went annually to fish for cod.

He would destroy them all at one fell swoop, cripple the Spanish marine for years, and leave the galleons to rot in the harbors for want of sailors to man them.

Had this been done, Philip of Spain would never have been able to threaten England with his " Invincible Armada." But the brave Englishmen of those days had to deal with a treacherous queen. The Hollanders who had engaged in a desperate struggle that they might have done with lies, and serve God with honesty and sincerity, were willing and eager to be annexed to England, and in union with her would have formed so strong a power as to be able to resist any Continental league against them.

But Elizabeth cared more for herself than for her country and her cause, and thus made warlike measures necessary which an Oliver Cromwell would have avoided.

Her duplicity may have provoked those republican ideas that were brought by Brewster and the other Pilgrim Fathers to America. Brewster was the friend and companion of Davison, Queen Elizabeth's Secretary of State, who was sent on an embassy to the Netherlands by her; and the contrast between these brave citizens and the treachery of the " good Queen Bess " must have given him a profound sense of the injury done to a great nation by the vices and follies of royalty.

The infamous manner in which the queen afterwards used her faithful secretary, Davison, as her scapegoat, and the sycophancy of Sandys, Archbishop of York, at Davison's mock trial, were strong arguments both against royalty and prelacy.

Under the cowardly, childish, and pedantic king who succeeded Elizabeth, Newfoundland was the bone of contention between the factions at his court, between Catholics and Protestants, and men who were neither, and men who were both.

Among the latter was the gallant Yorkshireman, Sir George Calvert, who was Secretary of State to James, but was compelled to resign his office in 1624, because he became a Catholic.

The British and Irish Catholics who came over seem to have been the men who came out to Newfoundland with the most honest intent of any,—to better themselves without injury to others, and to seek there "freedom to worship God" at a time when that freedom was denied in England, both to the Catholic and the Puritan. In 1620 Calvert had bought a patent conveying to him the lordship of all the south-eastern peninsula, which he called Avalon, the ancient name of Glastonbury in England.

He proposed to found there an asylum for the persecuted Catholics; and at a little harbor on the eastern shore, just south of Cape Broyle, which he called Verulam, a name since corrupted to Ferryland, he built a noble mansion, and spent altogether some $150,000, a much larger sum in those days than it seems now. But the site was ill chosen; and the imbecility of King James encouraged the French to attack the colony, so that at last Calvert wrote to Burleigh, "I came here to plant and set and sow, but have had to fall to fighting Frenchmen." He went home, and in the last year of his life he obtained a grant of land, which is now occupied by the States of Delaware and Maryland; and to its chief city his son gave the name of the wild Irish head-

land and fishing village, whence he took his own name of
Lord Baltimore in the Irish peerage.

After Calvert's departure, the Lord Lieutenant of Ireland sent out a number of settlers; and in 1638 Sir David
Kirke, one of the bravest of England's sea-captains, who
had taken Quebec, received from Charles I. a grant of all
Newfoundland, and settled at Verulam, or Ferryland, the
place founded by Calvert. Under Kirke the colony pros-
pered; but, as he took the part of Charles in the civil war,
his possessions were confiscated by the victorious Commonwealth.

At that time there were nearly two thousand settlers
along the eastern shore of Avalon; and the great Protector,
Oliver Cromwell, protected the rights of the Newfoundland
settlers as he did those of the Waldensians.

After his death came what Mr. Spearman calls the
"blots in the English history known as the reigns of
Charles II. and his deposed brother."

Mr. Spearman continues, "Frenchmen must understand
that no Englishman will for a moment accept as a precedent anything in those two reigns affecting the relations of
France and of England."

But here Mr. Spearman counts without his host. He
should recollect that the British government has, since the
death of Charles II., paid an annual pension to the Dukes
of Richmond simply because they were descended from the
Frenchwoman, Louise de la Querouaille, whose influence induced Charles II. to betray English interests to France,
and that but the other day the Salisbury government recog-
nized that precedent by paying the Duke of Richmond a
very large sum of money to buy off this infamous claim.
So long as the names of the Dukes of Richmond and
Saint Alban's (both descendants of Charles II.'s mistresses) remain on the roll of the British Peerage, the
Frenchman will have a right to laugh at Mr. Spearman's
claim; for we cannot ignore a precedent in our intercourse

with foreigners, so long as we act upon it in our domestic affairs.

Scarcely was Charles the Libertine seated on the throne of England, when the Frenchmen, in 1660, settled on the southern shore of Newfoundland, at a place which they called La Plaisance (now known as Placentia).

They were certainly either wiser or more fortunate in their choice of a location than the English: for, while St. John's and Ferryland, on the straight shore of Avalon, are exposed to the wildest gales of the Atlantic, and shut out by the arctic ice from all communication with the ocean for a part of the winter, Placentia is a protected harbor, open all the year round, and having a sheltered waterway navigable for the largest ships to the northernmost and narrowest part of the Isthmus of Avalon.

We must believe that the French would have managed Newfoundland better than the English if they had kept the island; for the men who cut the Isthmus of Suez would surely long ago have made a passage, three miles long, by which the ships of Trinity Bay might have found their way at the close of autumn to the safe winter harbors of the southern coast.

All along the southern shore the names on the map tell us of French occupation.

Port aux Basques, Harbor Breton, Rencontre Bay (called by the English Round Counter), Cape La Hune, Bay d'Espoir, are but a few of them.

The name which the English have given to this last is strangely characteristic. The Bay of Hope (Baie d'Espoir) of the French has been changed into the Bay of Despair of the English. It was really a Bay of Hope to the French; for from the head of one of its fiords, deep enough for the largest of our modern ships, an Indian trail goes northwards in less than 100 miles to the fertile valley of the Exploits River. Can we suppose that the French engineers would have allowed 200 years to elapse without

building a road along this trail? And yet not a single road
was built by the English conquerors before the year 1825;
and even to-day, to reach the point where the Indian trail
crosses the Exploits, we must travel 260 miles by rail from
Placentia or St. John's instead of 100 from Bay d'Espoir,
simply because the English holders of property in St.
John's, like dogs in the manger, will not permit any improve-
ment in the country, unless it can be made tributary to
their special interests.

That the English were worse enemies of Newfoundland
than the French, even in King Charles's time, may be seen
from the advice given by Sir Josiah Child, the chairman of
that great monopoly, the East India Company, that the
island "was to have no government, nor inhabitants permitted to reside at Newfoundland, nor any passengers or
private boat-keepers permitted to fish at Newfoundland."

The Lords of the Committee for Trade and Plantations
adopted the suggestion of Sir Josiah; and in 1676, just a
century before the American Declaration of Independence,
the west country adventurers began to drive away the resi-
dent inhabitants, and to take possession of their houses and
fishing stages, and did so much damage in three weeks that
Thomas Oxford declared 1,500 men could not make it good.

We should be unjust if we were to regard this infamous
dishonesty as simply an accident of the Restoration time.
Many of my American readers have doubtless heard of an
island called Ireland, which is much nearer to England
than Newfoundland. Lecky tells us how the English
land-owners, always foremost in selfishness, procured the
enactment of laws, in 1665 and 1680, absolutely prohibiting
the importation into England from Ireland of all cattle,
sheep, and swine, of beef, pork, bacon, and mutton, and
even of butter and cheese, with the natural result that the
French were enabled to procure these provisions at lower
prices, and their work of settling their sugar plantations
was much facilitated thereby.

In the Navigation Act of 1663 Ireland was deprived of all the advantages accorded to English ones, and thus lost her colonial trade; and, after the Revolution, the commercial influence, which then became supreme in the councils of England, was almost as hostile to Ireland as that of the Tory landlords. A Parliament was summoned in Dublin, in 1698, for the express purpose of destroying Irish industry; and a year later the Irish were prohibited from exporting their manufactured wool to any other country whatever. Prohibitive duties were imposed on Irish sail-cloth imported into England. Irish checked, striped, and dyed linens were absolutely excluded from the colonies, and burdened with a duty of 30 per cent. if imported into England. Ireland was not allowed to participate in the bounties granted for the exportation of these descriptions of linen from Great Britain to foreign countries. In 1698 two petitions, from Folkestone and Aldborough, were presented to Parliament, complaining of the injury done to the fishermen of those towns "by the Irish catching herrings at Waterford and Wexford, and sending them to the Straits, and thereby forestalling and ruining petitioners' markets"; and there was even a party in England who desired to prohibit all fisheries on the Irish shore except by boats built and manned by Englishmen.

Not only were the Irish prevented from earning money, but they were forced to pay large sums to the mistresses of English kings. Lecky tells us that the Duke of Saint Alban's, the bastard son of Charles II., enjoyed an Irish pension of £800 a year. Catherine Sedley, the mistress of James II., had another of £5,000 a year. William III. bestowed a considerable Irish estate on his mistress, Elizabeth Villiers. The Duchess of Kendall and the Countess of Darlington, two mistresses of the German Protestant · George I., had Irish pensions of the united value of £5,000. Lady Walsingham, daughter of the first-named of these mistresses, had an Irish pension of £1,500; and Lady

Howe, daughter of the second, had a pension of £500. Madame de Walmoden, mistress of the German Protestant King George II., had an Irish pension of £3,000. This king's sister, the queen dowager of Prussia, Count Bernsdorff, a prominent German politician, and a number of other German names may be found on the Irish pension list.

Lecky's description of the Protestant Church of Ireland is just as revolting. Archbishop Bolton wrote, "A true Irish bishop [meaning bishops of English birth and of the Protestant Church] has nothing more to do than to eat, drink, grow fat and rich, and die."

The English primate of Ireland ordained and placed in an Irish living a Hampshire deer-stealer, who had only saved himself from the gallows by turning informer against his comrades. Archbishop King wrote to Addison, "You make nothing in England of ordering us to provide for such and such a man £200 per annum, and, when he has it, by favor of the government, he thinks he may be excused attendance; but you do not consider that such a disposition takes up, perhaps, a tenth part of the diocese, and turns off the cure of ten parishes to one curate."

From the very highest appointment to the lowest, in secular and sacred things, all departments of administration in Ireland were given over as a prey to rapacious jobbers. Charles Lucas, M.P. for Dublin, wrote in 1761 to the Lord Lieutenant of Ireland, "Your excellency will often find the most infamous of men, the very outcasts of Britain, put into the highest employments or loaded with exorbitant pensions; while all that ministered and gave sanction to the most shameful and destructive measures of such viceroys never failed of an ample share in the spoils of a plundered people."

Arthur Young, in 1779, estimated the rents of absentee landlords alone at £732,000; and Hutchinson, in the same year, stated that the sums remitted from Ireland to Great

Britain for rents, interest of money, pensions, salaries, and
profit of offices amounted, on the lowest computation (from
1668 to 1773), to £1,110,000 yearly.

If, in treating of Newfoundland, I have made many extracts from Mr. Lecky's references to Ireland, it is in order
that I may show Mr. Spearman the danger of laying too
much stress on the French claims as the cause of the
present distress in England's oldest colony.

France had no claims in Ireland, and yet the conduct of
the British government and the British tradesman to that
unfortunate island is one of the blackest infamies of the
eighteenth century.

Mr. Lecky says in Chapter V., page 11, of his history:
"To a sagacious observer of colonial politics two facts were
becoming evident. The one was that the deliberate and
malignant selfishness of English commercial legislation was
digging a chasm between the mother country and the colonies which must inevitably, when the latter had become suf-
ficiently strong, lead to separation. The other was that the
presence of the French in Canada was an essential condition
of the maintenance of the British empire in America."

If Mr. Lecky had studied Newfoundland's history, he
might have added a third fact: namely, that the French
claims in Newfoundland have been for the Jingoes of the
last half-century a convenient means of excuse for shirking
their own responsibility to the unfortunate island, and for
covering up the malignant selfishness of those tradesmen
in Canada and England to whose private interests the
island has been sacrificed by the government.

It is interesting to observe how, at the time of the Peace
of Utrecht, on Article XIII. of which the modern claims of
France are based, the conditions were similar to those of
Tory intrigue to-day.

King Louis of France, encouraged by the momentary su-
premacy of the Tories in England, had insulted the English
people by recognizing the Pretender as King of England.

The popular indignation roused by this insult enabled
King William, by dissolving Parliament, to overthrow the
Tory power, and obtain a large majority pledged to war
with France. The Whigs carried this war to a victorious
conclusion ; but, most unfortunately for both England and
its colonies, Abigail Masham, by her influence over the
queen, secured the overthrow of the Whigs. And her cousin
Harley, a Tory, became Chancellor of the Exchequer, thus
permitting the Tories to reap the fruits of Whig victories.
In reference to the conclusion of the peace with France
Lecky says, " The tortuous proceedings that terminated in
the Peace of Utrecht form, beyond all question, one of the
most shameful pages in English history."

The greatest of England's generals was removed from the
head of the army, and replaced by a Tory of no military
ability. The allies of England were most basely deserted;
and a clause was inserted in the treaty respecting Newfoundland to the following effect : —

" But it is allowed to the subjects of France to practise
fishing and to dry fish on land in that part only which
stretches from the place called Bonavista to the Northern
Point of the said Island, and from thence, running down by
the Western Side, reaches as far as the place called Point
Riche."

What compensation was given by France in return for
this right to catch and dry fish on a part of the Newfoundland shore ?

That was the immense accession of guilty wealth acquired
by the Assiento Treaty, by which England obtained the
monopoly of the slave-trade to the Spanish colonies.

In the one hundred and six years from 1680 to 1786 England sent 2,130,000 slaves to America and the West Indies.

On this point Lecky writes : " It may not be uninterest-
ing to observe that, among the few parts of the Peace of
Utrecht which appear to have given unqualified satisfaction
at home, was the Assiento contract, which made of England

the great slave-trader of the world. *The last prelate who took a leading part in English* politics affixed his signature to the treaty. A Te Deum, composed by Handel, was sung in thanksgiving in the churches. Theological passions had been recently more vehemently aroused; and theological controversies had for some years acquired a wider and more absorbing interest in England than in any period since the Commonwealth. But it does not yet appear to have occurred to any class that a national policy, which made it its main object to encourage the kidnapping of tens of thousands of negroes, and their consignment to the most miserable slavery, might be at least as inconsistent with the spirit of the Christian religion as either the establishment of Presbyterianism or the toleration of prelacy in Scotland."

Is it not characteristic that, just as the Tories of Queen Anne's time were willing to prejudice the rights of a colony in return for the infamous profits of the slave-trade, so the Tory of 1862, Lord Robert Cecil, was among the chief Englishmen who sympathized with the slaveholders who were then attacking the American Union?

It is equally characteristic that this first of the Primrose Dames, Abigail Masham, quarrelled with her cousin Harley about the share which this lady of High Church principles was to receive out of the profits of the infamous trade.

Surely, the country that made so much profit out of the slave-trade is bound to compensate Newfoundland for the losses caused by its weakness in the French shore question rather than that France which in 1713 abandoned the infamous traffic to the British Tories.

The next treaty between France and England, that of Aix-la-Chapelle, in 1748, made no alteration in the Newfoundland question; but the government of England, in returning Louisbourg to the French, gave another of those proofs of the selfish indifference of the home government to the rights of the colonies which was one of the most potent causes that led the New Englanders, with the aid of France, to achieve their independence.

At the south-eastern extremity of Cape Breton Island the strong fortress of Louisbourg, which it was once the fashion to call the Gibraltar of America, threatened the safety of the New England and Newfoundland fisheries alike. Governor Shirley of Massachusetts induced the legislature to undertake an expedition against this fortress, and intrusted its command to Colonel William Pepperell. The New England forces, raw troops, commanded by untrained officers, astonished the world by capturing a fortress which was deemed impregnable. This was the most brilliant and decisive achievement of nine years of otherwise useless bloodshed and treachery.

It is well that the people of the United States propose to celebrate its one hundred and fiftieth anniversary this year; for, more than any other event in their colonial history, it gave them confidence in the power of untrained men of spirit to overcome the hireling soldiers of the European governments.

But the action of the British government at the Treaty of Aix-la-Chapelle, in restoring this fortress to the French, gave the colonists an equally necessary lesson. What did England get in exchange? The already mentioned Assiento, that famous compact which gave to England the right to ship slaves to the Spanish colonies, was confirmed for the four years it still had to run; and the fortress of Madras, which had been taken by the French in 1746, was restored to England in 1748 by the treaty. Even the most selfish and heartless of British politicians may doubt whether the true interests of his country were served by abandoning the American fortress for that of India; but the American statesman will not fail to see in the conduct of England towards her American colonists in this transaction a justification not alone for the Declaration of Independence, but also for that Monroe doctrine which, in its fullest application, will prevent the interference of any European power in the affairs of any part of America, not excluding Newfoundland. The Treaty of Paris, in 1763, which made Great

Britain practically master of North America, produced no change in the position of the 13,000 settlers then in Newfoundland. For them the London government cared nothing. The provisions of the treaty, by which France gave up Canada to England, only served to emphasize more strongly the injustice done by England to her Catholic population, both in Ireland and in Newfoundland.

In 1719 the Irish Privy Council, all tools of England, actually proposed to the London government that every unregistered priest or friar remaining in Ireland after the 1st of May, 1720, should be castrated; and, although the English ministers did not accept this suggestion, they adopted one that such priests should have a large P branded with a red-hot iron on their cheeks. It can be hardly wondered at that the more honest Irishmen sought refuge from such infamies either in foreign service or in the colonies, and many of them came to Newfoundland, only to find that the Church of England spirit of persecution was rampant there also.

Every government official was obliged to abjure the special tenets of Catholicism. In 1755 Governor Darrell commanded all masters of vessels who brought out Irish passengers to carry them back at the close of the fishing season. A special tax was levied on Roman Catholics, and the celebration of mass was made a penal offence. At Harbor Main, Sept. 25, 1755, the magistrates were ordered to fine a certain man £50 because he had allowed a priest to celebrate mass in one of his fishing-rooms. The room was ordered to be demolished, and the owner to sell his possessions and quit the harbor. Another who was present at the same mass was fined £20, and his house and stage destroyed by fire. Other Catholics, who had not been present, were fined £10 each, and ordered to leave the settlement. These infamies were not altered until the Tory government was humiliated by the victory of the United States and their allies. But even then the Newfoundland settlers were taught that England treats her loyal colonist more harshly than the possible rebel.

The Newfoundland settlers, Catholic or Protestant, had proved the most loyal men in the colony. When the French, under D'Iberville, captured St. John's, and all Newfoundland lay at their feet, the solitary exception was the little Island of Carbonear in Conception Bay, where the persecuted settler John Pynn and his gallant band still held aloft the British flag. In 1704–5 St. John's was again laid waste by the French, under Subercase; and, although Colonel Moody successfully defended the fort, the town was burned, and all the settlements about Conception Bay were raided by the French and their Indian allies. But Pynn and Davis bravely and successfully defended their island Gibraltar in Conception Bay.

In 1708 Saint Ovide surprised and captured St. John's, but again old John Pynn held the fort at Carbonear.

In the American War one of Pynn's descendants, a clerk at Harbor Grâce, raised a company of grenadiers from Conception Bay; and they fought with such success in Canada that he was knighted as Sir Henry Pynn, and raised to the rank of general. But the selfish government at home cared nothing for Newfoundland. The first Congress of the United States, Sept. 5, 1774, forbade all exports to the British possessions. This would not have hurt Newfoundland if the settlers had been allowed to carry on agricultural pursuits there. But these had always been discouraged by the English; and so they were dependent on the New England States for their supplies, and were threatened with absolute famine as soon as the war broke out. Had they been disloyal, they might have gained their rights from England; but their very loyalty to such a government was their worst misfortune.

Even in 1783 the Englishman had not learned the evil results of permitting royal interference in British politics. It is not merely in the reigns of the libertine kings that we see this. Queen Elizabeth injured England by interfering with the policy of its wisest statesmen. The ascendency of Harley and Saint John Bolingbroke, who deserted England's allies and threw away the fruits of Marlborough's victories, was due to the influence of a High Church waiting-woman over Queen Anne; and now, when even Lord North, to say nothing of the better class of Englishmen, disapproved of George III.'s obstinate resistance to the just claims of the American colonies. the support given to the king by the Tories led to the loss of a dominion far more valuable to England than all the trade of India or China.

He was obliged to call on a Liberal minister to undo, as far as possible, the evil done by himself and the Tories, just as in later days Mr. Gladstone had to settle with the United States the damage done by the Tories in the " Alabama" question.

The death of Rockingham left the direction of the negotiations with France and the United States in the hands of Lord Shelburne; and that he was extremely liberal in his arrangements with both countries was not to be wondered at. The wrong had been done by England; and the innocent English had to suffer, as well as the guilty ones. Unfortunately for Newfoundland, Shelburne did not cede this island to the United States; and so it had to bear more than its share in the misfortunes which the policy of King George had brought upon the British empire.

Mr. Spearman (page 411) writes that "Adams, the United States envoy, himself bred up among the New England fishermen, said 'he would fight the war all over again' rather than give up the ancestral right of the New Englanders to the Newfoundland fisheries"; but that Shelburne should be able, when France and America were victorious, to take away from the former power the concessions made to it by the Tories in 1713 and in 1763 was not to be expected.

There was a slight alteration in the shore line on which

the French might fish. They abandoned that right between
Cape Bonavista and Cape St. John, in consideration of
being allowed to catch and dry their fish along the shore
between Point Riche and Cape Ray. That was all; and
that is precisely the reason why the Beaconsfield-Salisbury
cabinet, in 1878, refused their sanction to the Bay St.
George Railroad.

The only advantage that the poor Newfoundlanders gained
from the war which caused them so much distress was the
fact that the English government was *whipped* into conced-
ing to their Roman Catholic population some of the rights
which for many years afterwards it obstinately withheld
from their brethren in Ireland.

In 1784 Vice-Admiral John Campbell, a man of liberal,
enlightened spirit, was appointed governor, and issued an
order that all persons inhabiting the island were to have
full liberty of conscience, and the free exercise of all such
modes of religious worship *as were not prohibited by law*.

In the same year the Rev. Dr. O'Donnell came out to
Newfoundland as its prefect apostolic. But the liberal
movement did not last long. Lord Shelburne retired, and
from 1784 till the passing of the Reform Bill in 1832 the
Tories mismanaged the affairs of Great Britain and her
colonies.

One great advantage of American independence was that
it gave the world a fair chance of judging between the results
of republican and royal government in colonial affairs.

We have certainly much that is rotten in the United
States; but, when we compare our republic at its worst with
British colonial administration, we can find good reason to
be thankful for the crowning mercy of 1781, when Washington, Lafayette, and De Grasse gained their decisive victory
over the troops of King George.

I will not now refer to England's use of her immense
power in India, China, and Japan. As I watched the course
of the Congress of Religions at Chicago in 1893, I could

not help thinking that the impressions taken from that Congress by our Oriental visitors would bear fruit that in due course may teach even his Grace, the Archbishop of Canterbury, something about England's criminal neglect of Christian duty to these people. For us it is enough to compare our position with that of the two unfortunate islands nearer our own shores, Ireland and Newfoundland.

Suppose we had been cursed with the rule of British Tories since 1783, is it likely that our condition would have been better than that of these islands?

Even such small instalments of justice as Mr. Gladstone has been able to secure through his splendid fight for "justice to Ireland" are due far more to the pressure exercised on England by the Irish in America than to British sense of right. Poor Newfoundland has had no Ireland in America to help her. She has been among the most loyal of England's colonies, and because of her loyalty she has been the most shamefully treated.

It might be expected that Irish Catholics would emigrate in large numbers to Newfoundland to escape the infamous penal laws by which King George oppressed them in Ireland, and that sailors from all parts of Great Britain would seek there a shelter from the press-gangs at home. Dr. O'Donnell, the first regularly authorized Catholic priest on the island, applied in 1790 for leave to build a chapel in an outport: and, the Tories being in power, Governor Milbanke replied: "The Governor acquaints Mr. O'Donnell [omitting the title of Rev.] that, so far from being disposed to allow of an increase of places of religious worship for the Roman Catholics of the island, he very seriously intends next year to lay those established already under particular restrictions. Mr. O'Donnell must be aware that it is not the interest of Great Britain to encourage people to winter in Newfoundland; and he cannot be ignorant that many of the lower order who would now stay would, if it were not for the convenience with which they obtain absolution here, go home

for it, at least once in two or three years.   And the Governor
has been misinformed, if Mr. O'Donnell, instead of advising
his hearers to return to Ireland, does not rather encourage
them to winter in this country.   On board the 'Salisbury,'
Nov. 2, 1790."

Do we need clearer proofs than that to show us who is
responsible for the misery both of Newfoundland and of
Ireland?   This Catholic priest, to whom the Tory governor
refuses both his religious rights and the titles given him by
his church and university, knew how to return good for evil.

In 1800 a mutinous plot was concocted among the soldiers
of the Royal Newfoundland Regiment to desert with their
arms, and, being joined by their friends outside, to plunder
St. John's, and afterwards escape to the United States.
Fortunately, Dr. O'Donnell, who had meanwhile become
bishop of St. John's, discovered the plot, and not only
warned the commanding officer, but exerted all his own
influence among the Catholics of the town to prevent an
outbreak.

The British government gave him the miserable pension
of £50 a year, while they pay one of £6,000 a year to
the Duke of Richmond, for no better reason than that he
was descended from the bastard son of that Louise de la
Querouaille who was the French mistress of King Charles II.

Chief Justice Reeves had been sent out from England
to report on the condition of the country: and his "History
of the Government of Newfoundland" shows that the
ascendency so long maintained by a mercantile monopoly
for narrow and selfish purpose had prevented the settlement
of the country, the development of its resources, and the
establishment of a proper system for the administration of
government.   Soon afterwards, in 1796, Admiral Waldegrave was appointed governor.   The merchants of Burin
complained to him that some of their fishermen wanted to
emigrate to Nova Scotia.   The merchants desired to prevent this.

Admiral Waldegrave reported thereon: "Unless these poor wretches emigrate, they must starve; for how can it be otherwise, while the merchant has the power of setting his own price on the supplies issued to the fishermen and on the fish that the people catch for him? Thus we see a set of unfortunate beings worked like slaves, and hazarding their lives, when at the expiration of their term (*however successful their exertions*) they find themselves not only without gain, but so deeply indebted as forces them to emigrate or drive them to despair." He further relates how the merchants refused to allow a tax of sixpence per gallon on rum, to help them to defray administrative expenses; and he describes the merchants as "opposed to every measure of government which a governor may think proper to propose for the general benefit of the island."

But even this Governor Waldegrave, though he so clearly saw the true cause of the evil, sternly refused the only remedy within reach, which was to grant the poor wretches the right to use the waste, uncultivated land which existed in so great abundance round about them.

He was so far from doing this that, when about to leave, he put on record, in 1799, for the use of his successor, that he had made no promise of any grant of land, save one to the officer commanding the troops, and that was not to be held by any other person. That is the way in which Britain's Tories have cared for her colonies.

Hatton and Harvey say: "In many of the smaller and more remote settlements successive generations lived and died without education and religious teaching of any kind. The lives of the people were rendered hard and miserable for the express purpose of driving them away. The governors of those days considered that loyalty to England rendered it imperative on them to depopulate Newfoundland."

How did England stand meanwhile towards the other nation, that of France, which had claims on Newfoundland?

This country had exercised its right to replace the Bourbons by the republic, just as England had replaced the Stuarts by the Guelphs.

But the Germans and Austrians had insolently interfered in the private affairs of France, and so made a military leader, in the person of Napoleon Bonaparte, absolutely indispensable for the protection of the country against foreign foes.

No sooner was Napoleon seated on the consular throne — he had not then become emperor — than he addressed a letter to King George III., urging the restoration of peace. "The war which has ravaged for eight years the four quarters of the globe, is it," he asks, "to be eternal?" "France and England," he concludes, "may, by the abuse of their strength, still for a time retard the period of their exhaustion; but I will venture to say the fate of all civilized nations is attached to the termination of a war which involves the whole world."

And what did England's Tory king answer? He intrusted the reply to Grenville, who was then the British minister for foreign affairs, and wrote to the Consul Bonaparte that, while his Britannic Majesty did not positively make the restoration of the Bourbons an indispensable condition of peace, nor claim to prescribe to France her form of government, he would intimate that only the one was likely to secure the other, and that he had not sufficient respect for her new ruler to entertain his proposals. Can we wonder that after so insolent a letter the first consul became emperor?

France is quite as proud as England; and the insolence of the Guelph, in presuming to insinuate that her first consul was not as good as he, was quite enough to provoke her into making the consul her emperor, and doing her best to chastise her insulters. Charles James Fox, in Parliament, pronounced the royal answer "odiously and absurdly wrong"; but the squires and borough-mongers of the House

of Commons supported the action of the king by a majority
of 265 to 64. It is for such infamies as this that Newfoundland has even to-day to bear all the inconveniences
of the French claims on their shores. I do not blame the
French for insisting that England shall scuttle out of Egypt
before she yields her claims in Newfoundland; but it is the
responsible English, and not the innocent Newfoundlanders,
who ought to pay the cost, and the conduct of England in
insisting that Newfoundland shall bear the burden is
cowardly and mean beyond all expression.

While the Tories were thus hurling England into war, it
is interesting to observe how the Guelphs conducted it.
The Duke of York, with a generalship worthy of his family,
led an army of British and Russian soldiers into a captivity
from which they could only be redeemed by the surrender
of prisoners taken on the sea by *real* Englishmen.

Englishmen were taxed in order to give the German
despots money wherewith to fight the French. Austria received for one campaign more money than England had to
pay even for the " Alabama " claims, and the czar of Russia
received £900,000 for the eight months his troops were
in the field. During the same war the king's second
son, the same Duke of York who had given so characteristic
a sample of Guelph generalship in leading his forces to
defeat, gave an equally characteristic specimen of Guelph
morality. He had for mistress one Mary Ann Clarke, a
woman of low origin, who transferred her intimacy to a
Colonel Wardle, and confided to him many of the secrets
of her relations to the royal duke. Wardle, on Jan. 27,
1809, affirmed in the House of Commons that the Duke of
York had permitted Mrs. Clarke to carry on a traffic in
commissions and promotions, and demanded a public
inquiry. Mrs. Clarke was examined at the bar of the
House of Commons for several weeks, displaying a shame-
less, witty impudence that drew continual applause and
laughter from a mob of English *gentlemen*, many of whom

knew her too well. The charges were proved, and the Duke of York resigned his position as commander-in-chief; and the disclosures made — doctors of divinity suing for bishoprics, and priests for preferment, at the feet of a harlot, kissing her palm with coin — may teach Englishmen what they have to guard against even to-day on the part of that Tory party that has religion, conscience, and morality much more on its lips than in its heart.

It is not altogether irrelevant in this connection to mention that in 1825, when the Catholic relief bill had passed the House of Commons by 268 votes against 241, the Duke of York opposed the repeal of the Catholic disabilities by the common Tory appeal to what they call conscience, saying "these were the principles to which he would adhere, and which he would maintain and act up to, to the latest moment of his life existence, whatever might be his situation in life, so *help him God.*"

England has indeed had to pay dearly for her hereditary monarchy, and for the awful hypocrisy which permits the appeal to God by such State Churchmen as the Duke of York to have any effect on politics. I need hardly say that the House of Lords did with the Catholic Emancipation Bill what it has lately done with the House of Commons Bill for Home Rule in Ireland, and threw it out.

While England was fighting France, she had also to fight the United States. It is an episode of which neither country has any reason to be proud. The New Englanders were mostly opposed to the declaration of war. The average Englishman knows little about it. He is taught by his history books that the victory of the "Shannon" over the "Chesapeake" destroyed the prestige of the American navy; and he is wrong even in that.

The "Shannon" had a brave and able commander, and had been many weeks at sea, so that Captain Broke had been able to train his men thoroughly, and, above all things, to prevent them from getting drunk.

Captain Lawrence had to engage many men who had never been on a war-vessel before, and did not know how to work the guns. Many of the sailors had bottles of rum in their pockets, and were too drunk to stand when their ship got within fighting distance of the " Shannon."

I wish our present Secretary of the Navy would learn the lesson, and now, when the need of the Newfoundlanders is so great, and when we require sober men to man our navy, give the brave fishermen of that island every reasonable inducement to enlist in our service.

The war closed unsatisfactorily, by the mediation of the Emperor Alexander of Russia; and the Treaty of Ghent left England mistress of the seas.

The treaties of 1814 and 1815 gave England another opportunity for relieving Newfoundland from the French control of her shore; but the Tories were at the helm, and became fellow-conspirators with other tyrants of Europe in perpetrating the most monstrous wrong and the completest restoration of despotism that was conceivable, in Germany, Austria, Italy, Spain, everywhere.

They insulted France by imposing upon her the rule of a Bourbon, and to this Bourbon they guaranteed those rights over Newfoundland on which the French republic bases its claims to-day.

Let us now turn to Newfoundland itself. While the nations were fighting, its merchants had enjoyed the monopoly of the cod-fisheries. Some of the capitalists had secured profits between £20,000 and £40,000 a year each, but they made the poor fishermen pay eight pounds a barrel for flour and twelve pounds a barrel for pork. They took their fortunes to England. No effort was made to open up roads or extend agriculture; for, if it had been done, the landlords of England would not have been able to sell their pork and wheat at such exorbitant prices there.

So, when the war ceased and other nations were enabled to compete in the fisheries, the colony had to pass through some years of disaster and suffering, while the merchants were spending their exorbitant profits in England.

The planters and fishermen had been in the habit of leaving their savings in the hands of the St. John's merchants. Many of these failed, and the hardly won money of the fishermen was swept away by the insolvency of their bankers. It is estimated that the working class lost a sum little short of £400,000 sterling.

Now, eighty years later, we have another instance of the same misfortunes, proceeding from the same cause,— the fact that the money made by the fishery has been taken off to England; that the banks, which are altogether in the hands of the mercantile, or English, party, have been unfaithful to their trust; and that the fishermen who hold the bankers' notes get, from the one bank, 80 cents, and, from the other, only 20 cents on the dollar.

The merchants applied for aid to the British government; and in June, 1817, a committee of the House of Commons met. The merchants had only two remedies to propose. One was the granting of a bounty, to enable them to compete with the French and the Americans, who were sustained by bounties; but, although England was a protectionist country at that time, it gave only bounties in favor of rich men, and not of the poor. The other was the deportation of the principal part of the inhabitants, now numbering 70,000, to the neighboring colonies.

The honest, sensible, easy plan, that of opening up the land to cultivation, so that the starving people might be able to grow their own food and breed their own cattle, was the one thing that these so-called practical Englishmen would not permit, because it might interfere with the profits of the British land-owner and merchant.

At that very time the local authorities of Massachusetts were giving a bounty for each Newfoundland fisherman brought into the State.

When Sir Thomas Cochrane was made governor in 1825,

his government made the first road in the island. For one hundred and forty-five years England had been master of the island, and not a single road had been built suitable for wheeled carriages. Is it conceivable that the French would so completely have neglected the colony if they had been its masters?

In 1832, when the Reform Bill put an end to the malign influence of Tory ascendency in England, Newfoundland also gained the boon of representative government; but it was only a merchants' government. The people who elected the House of Assembly did not dare to vote against the will of the merchants for fear of losing employment; and, while their representatives had the power of debating, passing measures, and voting moneys. the Council, which was composed of nominees of the crown, selected exclusively from the merchant class, could throw out all their measures, and were irresponsible to the people.

In England King George IV. had rendered only one service to the people,— he had brought royalty into contempt, and so strengthened the feeling which resulted in the passage of many necessary measures which his father and brothers had opposed. But the selfish interests of the merchants and land-owners of England were still in the way of many reforms. Benjamin Disraeli, who did his worst to prevent the starving people from having cheap bread, became the flunkey and afterward the master of the Tory squires; and it was not until thousands had died of famine in Ireland that the selfish land-owners agreed to that reduction of duty on grain which made free trade so popular in England.

Now, by a wise colonization policy, the government might have helped both Ireland and Newfoundland.

By passing a law to the effect that, so long as the French gave a bounty on the export of salt fish, the English government would give their own fishermen exactly the same amount of protection, the French would soon have been brought to terms; and, by opening up Newfoundland to settlement by roads and railways, many of the starving Irish would have been provided with homes under the British flag far more comfortable than any that they could find in their native land. So a more prosperous Ireland would have risen on this side of the Atlantic, and England would have gained thereby. The Irish and the Catholic were really quite as loyal to the empire as any others. The difference was that the English High Churchman and the Scotch Presbyterian got all the privileges; and the Irishman and the Catholic were taught by the action of the British government that insurrection was their only hope of getting simple justice.

India, China, Newfoundland, Ireland, were simply sweaters' dens for the profit of England and Scotland.

Just as in Newfoundland the British merchant insisted on keeping out every trace of free trade that would enable the poor fisherman to sell his fish in the highest market and buy his provisions in the lowest, so in China the British in 1838 insisted on forcing the Chinaman to buy the poisonous opium of India, although in 1834 the China government had warned the British of their intention to prohibit the infamous traffic. The war that England thereupon proclaimed against China was one of the most infamous and cowardly of the century, and made British Christianity more hateful even than its opium to the rulers of the Celestial Empire. £4,375,000 was extorted from the Chinese emperor for the expenses of the war ($20,000,000), and £1,250,000 ($5,000.000) for the opium which, with perfect justice, he had confiscated from the smugglers. The mob of London cheered the wagons which brought the ill-gotten treasure through the streets; and the mob in Parliament thanked the officers who had murdered the helpless and unoffending Chinese, while the parsons congratulated the people on the opening of China to British commerce, British civilization, and British religion.

The brutalizing influence of this method of carrying on

the foreign trade of England was shown by a later altogether unnecessary war with China about the Lorcha
"Arrow." This was a Chinese pirate vessel, which had obtained, by false pretences, the temporary possession of
the British flag. On Oct. 8, 1856, the Chinese police
boarded it in the Canton River, and took off twelve China-
men on a charge of piracy. This they had a perfect right
to do; but the British consul, Mr. Parkes, instead of thank-
ing them, demanded the instant restoration of men who had
been flying a British flag under false pretences. He applied to Sir John Bowring, the British plenipotentiary at
Hong Kong, for assistance. Sir John was an able and
experienced man. He had been editor of the *Westminster
Review*, had a bowing, if not a speaking acquaintance with
a dozen languages, had been one of the leaders of the free
trade party, and had a thorough acquaintance with the
Chinese trade. For many years he had been secretary of
the Peace Society.

He was the author of several hymns. In fact, an American hymn-book contains not less than seventeen from his
pen. One of them, found in most modern hymn-books, was
that commencing,—

"In the cross of Christ I glory";

and its author proceeded to glory in the cross of the Prince
of Peace by making war on the Chinese, although the governor, Yeh, had sent back all the men whose return was
demanded by Mr. Parkes.

Mr. Justin McCarthy, in his "History of our own Times,"
says, "During the whole business Sir John Bowring con-
trived to keep himself almost invariably in the wrong; and,
even where his claim happened to be in itself good, he
managed to assert it in a manner at once untimely, impru-
dent, and indecent."

One of the highest legal authorities in England, Lord
Lyndhurst, declared Sir John Bowring's action, and that of

the British authorities who aided him, to be unjustifiable on any principle either of law or reason; and Mr. Cobden, himself an old friend of Sir John Bowring, moved in the House of Commons that "the papers which have been laid upon the table fail to establish satisfactory grounds for the violent measures resorted to at Canton in the late affair of the 'Arrow.'"

Nearly all the best men in the House of Commons — Gladstone, Roundell Palmer, Sydney Herbert, Milner Gibson, Sir Frederick Thesiger, as well as many of the chief Tories — supported Mr. Cobden; and the vote of censure was carried against Lord Palmerston's government by 263 to 247. But Lord Palmerston, then the hero of the Evangelical Church party,—"Palmerston, the true Protestant." "Palmerston, the only Christian Prime Minister,"--knew exactly the strength of British Christianity when it interfered with the sale of British beer, or Indian opium, or Manchester cotton, and appealed to the shop-keeper instincts of the British people. He dissolved Parliament; and Cobden, Bright, Milner Gibson, W. J. Fox, Layard, and many others were left without seats. Manchester rejected John Bright because he had spoken in the interests of peace and honor, and condemned one of the most cowardly, brutal, and unprovoked wars of the century.

We see the same cause at work in Ireland. One British bishop, Dr. Thirlwall, of St. David's, had the manliness to favor Mr. Gladstone's bill for the disestablishment of the Irish Church; but most of them acted in this matter in direct opposition to the teachings of Him whom they profess to worship as their God. Mr. John Bright warned the Lords that, by throwing themselves athwart the national course, they might meet with "accidents not pleasant to think of"; and there is no doubt that the warning had its effect. And even now I do not think that the people of Ireland will ever get from the House of Lords that measure of right which even the House of Commons has unwillingly and grudgingly accorded to them, unless the Irishmen of America come to their aid in a more effective manner than they have ever yet done.

Newfoundland, unlike Ireland, has few friends in the United States, and therefore is wholly at England's mercy. What it suffered in the past I have already told. Let us see how England has treated it in the last few years.

It was from Lord Palmerston, of all men, that the Newfoundlander might hope for redress.

He had said in the Don Pacifico case, "As the Roman in the days of old held himself free from indignity when he could say, 'Civis Romanus sum,' so also a British subject, in whatever land he be, shall feel confident that the watchful eye and the strong arm of England shall protect him against injustice and wrong."

Surely, the 200,000 Newfoundlanders had more right to expect that Lord Palmerston would maintain this principle in their defence than the extortionate Portuguese Jew or the Chinese pirates who were taken from the Lorcha "Arrow."

And Lord Palmerston had the best opportunity of helping the Newfoundlander; for he was the intimate friend of Louis Napoleon and Persigny. By his approbation of Louis Napoleon's *coup d'état* he became the creator of the Anglo-French Alliance; and, since this alliance was a matter of life and death to the Second Empire, he might have used the opportunity, after the Crimean War, of exercising such pressure upon Louis Napoleon as to secure justice to Newfoundland.

But he neglected it, and thereby he lost the opportunity of strengthening the position of England and Canada towards the United States at the time of the "Trent" and "Alabama" affairs.

We may be glad of this; but, from a British point of view, it was not merely an injustice to Newfoundland, but also a political blunder.

One would suppose that, simply as a matter of imperial

policy, the British government would long ago have built
a railroad across this island, in order to have the quickest
possible connection with its Canadian dependency. The
Fenian raids into Canada, the Confederate raids from
Canada, the Red River Rebellion, the possibility of war
arising from the " Trent " incident, the necessity of securing
a rapid means of communication with the Pacific, should
all, on purely strategic grounds, have induced the British
government to establish a safe naval station in some southern harbor of Newfoundland, with a railroad communication
to the west shores of the island.

But the government left the Newfoundlanders, impover-
ished by the consequences of British misrule, to take the
initiative; and it was not until 1878 that they were able to
do anything. Then the Hon. William V. Whiteway induced
the Newfoundland government to offer an annual subsidy
of $120,000 per annum and liberal grants of crown lands to
any company which would construct and operate a railway
across Newfoundland, connecting by steamers with Britain
or Ireland on the one hand, and the Intercolonial and Canadian lines on the other. Of the immense advantage of such
a line to Great Britain, constructed as it would be at the
expense of Newfoundland, I need hardly speak, and every
patriotic ministry would have greeted the proposal with en-
thusiasm; but, most unfortunately both for England and
for Newfoundland, the Premier was Mr. Disraeli, and the
Foreign Secretary Lord Salisbury. What Lord Salisbury
was may be learned from Mr. James G. Blaine's account of
his speeches and conduct as Lord Robert Cecil in 1862.
I know of no sermon preached within the last thirty years
that inculcates a more necessary moral and religious lesson
for Lords and Commons and parsons of England than that
taught in the twentieth chapter of the Hon. James G.
Blaine's " Twenty Years of Congress." From it we may
learn, first of all, that the right of secession of Ireland or
Newfoundland from the British empire is already virtually

conceded by many of the Tory leaders of England. Mr.
Blaine gives us in that chapter a list of twenty-four members
of the British House of Commons, ten members of the
British Peerage, one admiral, one vice-admiral, one captain, one colonel, one lieutenant colonel, and a host of
knights and baronets who subscribed money to the Confederate Cotton Loan, while he gives extracts from the
speeches of Bernal Osborne, Lord John Russell, Lord
Palmerston, Mr. Gregory, M.P., Mr. G. W. Bentinck, M.P.,
Lord Robert Cecil, now Marquis of Salisbury, M. Lindsy,
M.P., Lord Campbell, Earl Malmesbury, Mr. Laird, M.P.
(the builder of the "Alabama" and the rebel rams), Mr.
Horsman, M.P. for Stroud, the Marquis of Clanricarde
(a name familiar to all Irishmen from its connection with
the evictions), Mr. Peacocke, M.P., Mr. Clifforde, M.P., Mr.
Haliburton, M.P., Lord Robert Montague, Sir James Ferguson, the Earl of Donoughmore, Mr. Alderman Rose, Lord
Brougham, and the Right Hon. William Ewart Gladstone,
Chancellor of the Exchequer, breathing hostility to the
cause of the Union States and friendship for the slaveholder ; while the few honest men in the House of Commons, who, like John Bright, Foster, Charles Villiers, Milner
Gibson, and Cobden, spoke for the cause of the North,
were reviled, not alone by their colleagues, but even by
many of their constituents, because they defended the side
of liberty, truth, and justice.

Why should we withhold from the just cause of Ireland
and Newfoundland the sympathy which England gave to
the secessionist slaveholder?

Of course the London *Times* was on the slaveholder's
side. On the last day of December, 1864, it said that "Mr.
Seward and other teachers and flatterers of the multitude
still affect to anticipate the early restoration of the Union ":
and in three months from that date the rebels were con-
quered.

It was on March 7, 1862, that Lord Robert Cecil said in

Parliament: "The plain fact is that the Northern States of America can never be our sure friends, because we are rivals politically, rivals commercially, We aspire to the same position. We both aspire to the government of the seas. We are both manufacturing people, and in every port as well as at every court we are rivals of each other. . . . With the Southern States the case is entirely reversed. The people are an agricultural people. They furnish the raw material of our industry, and they consume the products which we make from it. With them, therefore, every interest must lead us to cultivate friendly relations; and we have seen that, when the war began, they at once recurred to England as their natural ally."

It was easy enough for the most cowardly man, in Lord Robert Cecil's position, to use such words, even were he naught more than a lath painted over to imitate steel. Even if England is ruined, he is safe. But it was quite another matter when, sixteen years later, the poor Newfoundlander applied to him and Disraeli-Beaconsfield for the right to build a railroad.

Russia had just declared her intention of demolishing the last unpleasant clause in the treaty forced upon her by France and England at the close of the Crimean War; and Russia was a more dangerous foe than the Northern States. And the story of the Beaconsfield-Salisbury connection with that affair excited the laughter of all other diplomatists in Europe.

They pretended to have brought peace with honor from the Conference of Berlin. But what did the rest of Europe think about it?

It made the Christian populations of the South believe that Russia was their especial friend, and their enemies were England and the unspeakable Turk; it strengthened among the Greeks the impression already made by Palmerston's action in the Don Pacifico case,—that France was their friend, and England their enemy; and it created everywhere the impression that the Congress was a theatrical piece of business, merely enacted as a pageant on the Berlin stage.

England has not yet paid the full penalty of her stupid acquiescence in the rule of Disraeli and Salisbury; and it will cost her yet far more than she paid for the results of Tory infamy and Whig senility in the "Alabama" business, for she has enemies to deal with who are far less generous and far slyer than the people of the United States. It was under the Beaconsfield-Salisbury cabinet that Sir Bartle Frere made that infamous declaration of war against Cetewayo which led to the defeat of Lord Chelmsford's British troops by a lot of half-naked savages. It was under this ministry that the stupid expedition to Afghanistan led to the massacre of Sir Louis Cavagnari and the members of his staff. It was under this ministry that the soul-stirring anthem of Thompson,

> "When Britain first at Heaven's command,"

was superseded by the rant of the Tory street-walker,—

> "We don't want to fight;
> But, by jingo, if we do,
> We've got the ships, we've got the men,
> We've got the money, too,"

And the manner in which the government used the ships, the men, and the money, proved that there was one thing needful which the Jingoes had not got; and that is manhood.

To this Jingo ministry it was, then, that Sir William V. Whiteway had to apply for the imperial sanction to the railway; and sanction was *refused*. For what reason? The *pretended reason* was that the western terminus of the line at Bay St. George would be on that part of the coast affected by the French treaty rights. It may be open to doubt whether the French claims which interfered with the establishment of a railroad terminus at Bay St. George

were just or not ; but there is not the slightest doubt that
Lord Palmerston, in his note of July 10, 1838, to Count
Sebastiani, had maintained that they were not justified, and
that the Tories were and are of the same opinion.

But when a whole colony of Englishmen were wronged
according to the statements both of Palmerston and Salisbury, the Beaconsfield-Salisbury administration *dare* not
maintain the rights of these Englishmen against the French.
That is the courage and the bravery of British Jingoism,
which bullies weak China and little Greece in support of a
Sir John Bowring or a Don Pacifico, but dares not maintain
an Englishman's rights against the French republic.

The question might easily have been settled without
offending France by making Port aux Basques, which is
less than eighty miles south-west of Bay St. George and
beyond the French treaty limits, the terminus of the line.

There must, then, have been some concealed reason
behind the pretended one. It is absolutely certain that
there were two influences at work in London which were
directly antagonistic to the true interest both of Great
Britain and Newfoundland. One was that of the Canadian
party, who are determined to boycott every scheme that
would make any Newfoundland port a rival of Halifax.
The other is the British, or mercantile, party, who for two
hundred years past have consistently and successfully opposed the introduction of any industry into the island that
would enable the fishermen to escape from their present
bondage.

If either Beaconsfield or Salisbury had really cared for
England's interests, they must have foreseen that, even if
they were willing to sacrifice Newfoundland, the position
they took in this matter must in the highest degree be
damaging to the European prestige of Great Britain.
When republican France was threatened by all the tyrants
of Europe, the terrible Danton said, " Il nous faut de
l'audace, et encore de l'audace, et toujours de l'audace."

To-day the Frenchman requires no Danton to teach him the lesson; for the extraordinary confession of weakness made by the Jingo government of 1878 in refusing to sanction a line that could have been built without touching the French shore question at all was a direct encouragement to the French to persevere in that policy which they have since so successfully pursued in Madagascar, in Siam, in Africa, and in Newfoundland.

No matter whether the French claims in Newfoundland be right or wrong, the Beaconsfield-Salisbury government have practically surrendered the matter; and the only thing left for the British government is to compensate Newfoundland for its loss, as America was compensated for the "Alabama" damages. But they will not do it.

Mr. Whiteway had to find another means of helping the colony. He was obliged to choose between two alternatives,—either to build no railway at all or only one which would avoid the very districts which, for the benefit of the settler, ought to be opened for settlement.

So the line to Harbor Grace was built. But even this the wealthy British did not build. It was left to an American syndicate. P. T. McG., writing of this line to the New York *Weekly Post* of Jan. 2, 1895, says, "The contract was given to an enterprising Yankee, who built a few miles, swindled the shareholders, fleeced the colony, and then decamped, leaving as a legacy an unfinished road, an interminable lawsuit, and a damaged colonial credit."

I happen to know another side of the question; and it does not become the Englishmen interested in that railway matter to talk of "Yankee swindlers."

When Sir Robert Thorburn became Premier of Newfoundland, he took the first step necessary to make this line of some value to the tax-payers by extending it twenty-seven miles to Placentia, the old French "La Plaisance." This line was of immense value to St. John's, because it gave the people of that city a convenient winter harbor which is always open, by which they have an easy communication with Canada and the United States; and I hope the time will soon come when we shall have steamers running from Boston, touching at the French Island of St. Pierre, and then going to Placentia.

What were the English diplomatists doing meanwhile? In 1890 they were arranging a *modus vivendi* with the French government about the lobster fisheries. The Tories were in power, and Sir James Ferguson was the Under-secretary of State. This gentleman's sentiments towards the United States have been recorded by the Hon. James G. Blaine. In his "Twenty Years of Congress," Vol. II., page 481, foot-note, he writes: Sir James Ferguson declared in the House of Commons, March 14, 1864, that "wholesale peculations and robberies have been perpetrated under the form of war by the generals of the Federal States; and worse horrors than, I believe, have ever in the present century disgraced European armies have been perpetrated under the eyes of the Federal government, and yet remain unpunished. These things are as notorious as the proceedings of a government which seems anxious to rival one despotic and irresponsible power of Europe in its contempt for the public opinion of mankind." These words need no commentary to-day. They show us pretty clearly the character of the man who then spoke them, and will prepare us for his treatment of the Newfoundland question. On March 20, 1890, he made the following statement in the House of Commons: —

"The Newfoundland government was consulted as to the terms of the *modus vivendi, which was modified to some extent to meet their views;* but it was necessary to conclude it without referring it to them in its final shape."

Five days later the Governor of Newfoundland telegraphed to the Secretary of State: —

"My ministers request that incorrect statement made by Under-secretary of State for foreign affairs be immediately contradicted, *as the terms of modus vivendi were not modified in accordance with their views.* Ministers protested against any claims of French, and desired time to be changed till January for reasons given ; but that was ignored, and *modus vivendi* entered into without regard to their wishes. Ministers much embarrassed by incorrect statement made by Under-secretary of State."

Of course the Secretary of State supported the statement of Sir James Ferguson, and refused to correct it. But on page 54 of the case for the colony, published June. 1890, we find the words : —

"Two facts are placed beyond dispute by the above-quoted correspondence: (1) that the consent of the 'community' of Newfoundland to the *modus vivendi* was not obtained by laying it before the legislature, which the 'Labouchere' despatch declared to be the proper action to be taken in such cases ; (2) and that even the government of Newfoundland was not consulted as to the adoption of the *modus vivendi* as settled."

The Labouchere despatch alluded to above, and called by the Newfoundlanders their "Magna Charta," had been sent by the Right Hon. Henry Labouchere on March 26, 1857. But Mr. Labouchere was not a Tory; and there is the whole difference. So Newfoundland still has to suffer for the criminal negligence which British Tories have displayed from 1713 until to-day.

There was one Englishman, and that the Governor of Newfoundland itself, who had a clear and honorable notion of the imperial government's duty to its unfortunate colony. Sir G. William des Vœux, writing from the government House, St. John's, Jan. 14, 1887, to the Colonial Office in London, after reciting the circumstances, says : "If this be so, as indeed there are other reasons for believing, I would respectfully urge that in fairness the heavy resulting loss should not, or, at all events, not exclusively, fall upon this colony, and that if in the national interest a right is to be withheld from Newfoundland which naturally belongs to it, and the possession of which makes to it all the difference between wealth and penury, there is involved on the part of the nation a corresponding obligation to grant compensation of a value equal or nearly equal to that of the right withheld."

Nothing can be fairer than that, and it is written by the trusted official of the British government.

Sir G. William des Vœux continues, "In conclusion, I would respectfully express on behalf of this suffering colony the earnest hope that the vital interests of 200,000 British subjects will not be disregarded out of deference to the susceptibilities of any foreign power," etc.

The best interests of those 200,000 inhabitants can be served without touching the French shore at all. Even if France concedes all that Newfoundland demands, the bounty question is in the way; and Newfoundland cannot compete with that.

France gives this bounty — and quite rightly — as a protection to her sailors. A similar protection to England's fishermen would not be permitted by the Manchester men.

The other way is to build a railroad connecting the mining and agricultural districts along the French shore with Port aux Basques. Of course I do not mean such railroads as are built in England. They have been taxed to the extent of more than seventy millions of pounds sterling over and above the real value of the land sold to them by the rapacious land monopolists. They have been taxed to the extent of many millions more for legal expenses, which, if the House of Commons were equal to its duties, could have been saved. They have been taxed in many cases to find sinecure berths for the dependants of rich men; and so, in order to pay a fair dividend to their stockholders, they must reduce wages to the lowest point, and screw the utmost penny out of their customers.

It is, then, the American way which I recommend as a

model, and which the Newfoundland government have tried
to imitate in their contract with Mr. Reid, of Montreal.
They could have made a far more advantageous contract
with him if England had done her duty; but neither Mr.
Reid nor Newfoundland is to be blamed for England's
fault.

The contract signed on May 16, 1893, by Mr. R. G.
Reid binds him to construct a line about five hundred miles
in length, connecting Placentia Junction and the chief eastern ports of Newfoundland with Port aux Basques, and to
operate this line as well as the Placentia Branch Railway
for a period of ten years, commencing Sept. 1, 1893.
After that the line is to become the property of the Newfoundland government, and will be an interesting experi-
ment in the State ownership of railroads. For every mile
of single 42-inch gauge built by Mr. Reid he is to
receive the sum of $15,600 in Newfoundland government
bonds, bearing interest at $3\frac{1}{2}$ per cent., and eight square
miles of land. The increase in rental value of this land
will give a large revenue, even if the line should not pay
its working expenses.

The land grant for 500 miles of railroad would amount
to 2,500,000 acres. If Newfoundland were one of the
United States, capital enough would be subscribed to
enable Mr. Reid to finish his contract in the allotted time;
but, as it is under England, and must therefore suffer from
the awful burden of England's diplomatic incapacity, capital
holds aloof from it.

Where does British money go? The Tory of 1878
sang,—

> " We don't want to fight;
> But, by jingo, if we do,
> We've got the ships, we've got the men,
> We've got the money, too."

It is interesting to see how that money, which is withheld from Britain's oldest colony, has been spent.

We will begin with Mr. Blaine's "Twenty Years of Congress." On page 479 he quotes Lord Campbell as saying in Parliament on March 23, 1863, "Swelling with omnipotence, Mr. Lincoln and his colleagues dictate insurrection to the slaves of Alabama." (That fatal word, "Alabama"! Will it ever cease to trouble the British conscience?) And he spoke of the administration as "ready to let loose 4,000,000 negroes on their compulsory owners, and to renew from sea to sea the horrors and crimes of San Domingo." Mr. Blaine says, further, that Lord Campbell argued earnestly in favor of the British government joining the government of France in acknowledging Southern independence. He boasted that within the last few days a Southern loan of £3,000,000 sterling had been offered in London, and of that £9,000,000, or three times the amount, had been subscribed.

Here, then, we have a means of accounting for $15,000,000. Another $15,000,000 is accounted for by the money which America forced England to pay for the "Alabama" depredations. On that point Mr. Laird, the builder of the "Alabama," deserves to be immortalized. According to Mr. Blaine, on March 27, 1863, Mr. Laird was loudly cheered in the House of Commons when he declared that "the institutions of the United States are of no value whatever, and have reduced the name of liberty to an utter absurdity."

Another large lump of Jingo money has gone into the Russian loan; and, of this loan, $4,000,000 is coming to Bethlehem in Pennsylvania. O shade of John Roebuck, look back to the earth you have left, and see what your words have done for the armor plate manufacturers of your Sheffield constituency. While still among us in the flesh, you said on April 23, 1863, on some trouble: "It may lead to war; and I, speaking for the English people, am prepared for war. I know that language will strike the heart of the peace party in this country, but it will also strike the heart of the insolent people who govern America."

And on June 30. 1863, you said : " The South will never come into the Union ; and, what is more, I hope it never may. I will tell you why I say so. America while she was united ran a race of prosperity unparalleled in the world. Eighty years made the republic such a power that, if she had continued as she was a few years longer, she would have been the great bully of the world.

"As far as my influence goes, I am determined to do all I can to prevent the reconstruction of the Union. . . . I say, then, that the Southern States have indicated their right to recognition. They hold out to us advantages such as the world has never seen before. I hold that it will be of the greatest importance that the reconstruction of the Union *should not take place.*"

The United States have given England the war you hoped for,— not a war against soldiers and sailors, who, unlike those who followed Colonel Pepperell and Washington and Isaac Hull and Grant and De Grasse to victory, require the protection of a contagious diseases act, but a war of protective tariffs.

The State which gave its name to the pirate ship " Alabama " now votes for tariffs to exclude the iron, steel, and coal of England. Sheffield is in sackcloth and ashes because Pennsylvania has taken away from her the Russian order for armor plates, and countless millions of British dollars are invested in American factories, giving high wages to tariff-protected American workmen instead of sweaters' wages to the beer-sodden lunatics who sing to your honor the Tory strain,—

> " By jingo, if we do,
> We've got the ships, we've got the men,
> We've got the money, too."

In almost every case in which a British investor has lost his money in the United States it can be proved that some

British expert or financial agent earned a large sum by inducing him to invest.

At any rate, these immense investments in American railroads, loans, and lands, have one great advantage for the
United States. They bind over England to keep the peace
toward us. There is no more unpatriotic, no more unmoral,
no more cowardly man than the British financial agent and
money-lender. If only the security is good, he will rather
lend money at $4\frac{1}{8}$ per cent. for the most devilish than at 4
per cent. for the most divine purpose. It is due to the influence of the money-lending class that England has so
completely lost the grip of heart and brain on her imperial
duties.

It is said that John Bull pays a tax of $700,000,000 a
year to the liquor interest, to say nothing of the indirect
damages resulting from the fact that the liquor interest is
the chief supporter of the brothel, the baccarat table, and
the Tory Democracy. The beerage has proved of late
years also a highway to the peerage; and it has also served
to deplete the pockets of a good many British fools, who
were misled into the insane delusion that they could earn
as much from the profits of American guzzling as from
those of British beer-drinking. America has been infested
for some time by a crowd of Englishmen, who came here
hunting options on American breweries, which they sold at
a high price to their English dupes. In one case some
breweries, which cost the owners less than $2,000,000,
were sold in England for $6,000,000, the Englishmen and
Americans who managed the transaction making enormous
profits at the expense of their dupes.

On investigating the published accounts of some twelve
American brewery companies in which Englishmen have
been induced to invest more than $41,808,000, I find that
the depreciation in selling price of shares, taking the highest rates of November, 1894, was no less than $21,917,280,
or 52.42 per cent. on the paid-up capital; and, taking the

common stock alone, the loss exceeds over seventy per
cent. on the paid-up capital.

I am glad of it. The Englishman who, knowing the
influence of this infernal traffic on his own countrymen,
would make money by extending its curse to the United
States, deserves to lose his money quite as much as the
Tory investors in the Confederate Loan deserved their
loss. Now suppose this $70,000,000 thus invested in
"Alabama damages," Confederate Loan, and American
breweries had been put into Newfoundland roads and
railways, what would have been the result? An immense
amount of traffic which now must pay toll to American
railroads would have gone over purely British lines, all
the way through British America to China and Japan.
All the mining and agricultural lands of Newfoundland
might have been developed. The French shore question
would have ceased to occupy the diplomatic wiseacres,
because the people would have found so much profit in
other employments as to care nothing about French com-
petition in the cod and lobster fishery. Newfoundland
itself would have become an impregnable arsenal for the
British navy, commanding the entrances to the St. Lawrence, and, in case of war with the United States, giving
that navy the power of practically blockading all the
Atlantic coast.

All this has been thrown away, because the British Jingo
supports a Tory cabinet, which, while making theatrical
demonstrations of imperialism, neglects imperial duties and
betrays imperial interests.

And look even at sober free trade Manchester, the community which is supposed to understand the worth of money
better than any other in the world. Has it really gained by
its Jingo policy? Professing to be the stronghold of free
trade, it rejected the great free-trader, John Bright, when
in Sir John Bowring's war he asked for justice to China.
It rejected Mr. Gladstone when he sought the suffrages of

South-east Lancashire that he might relieve Ireland from the insolent domination of an alien church.

And now the great makers of cotton machinery are coming from Lancashire to establish factories in New England, and her spinning and weaving mill corporations are losing their markets and their profits. Of eighteen such corporations whose shares are quoted in the *Economist*, the highest November prices of common stock show a loss of $2,553,294 on the paid-up capital. Supposing that, instead of supporting the Jingoes, Manchester had sent men to Parliament who would support a wise and conservative policy in the colonies, Newfoundland included, would it not have been better for her interests, to say nothing of principle?

The Newfoundlanders in Boston, Mass., held a public meeting there on the 16th of February, at which the Rev. Frederick Woods, their chairman, said: "If we could only take our old island, and lay her at the feet of Uncle Sam! I wish we could." And every suggestion of annexation to the United States was applauded by the Newfoundlanders present.

The Newfoundlanders on the island desire annexation just as much, but they dare not say so, for they are starving; and those who venture to suggest separation from England would be punished by the withdrawal of charity, if not by even sterner means.

They are justified in their desire; for England has been disloyal to them, and holds the island by no better right than that by which Turkey holds Armenia.

Let that England, who expects every man to do his duty, do her own. Let her, first of all, relieve the suffering.

Second. Let her press on the completion of the railroad at English expense to Port aux Basques as quickly as possible, and subsidize a mail line between England and the American Continent by way of a Newfoundland port, holding the railroad property as security for money expended.

Third. Let her modify her fiscal system so as to give a real *free trade*, not only to the Newfoundland fisherman, but also to those of Great Britain and Ireland, so that the foreigner shall not be able to deprive British subjects either of their home or foreign markets. A small import duty on all fish imported into the British Isles, except from Newfoundland, and a bounty on the exports equal to that given by France, will suffice.

Fourth. Let her aid the unfortunate victims of her Lord Clan-Rackrents to find comfortable farms and holdings in those parts of the French shore and along the railroad which are suitable for settlement.

If she does this, she may derive some comfort from at least one passage in her Prayer Book,— " When the wicked man turneth away from the wickedness that he has committed, and doeth that which is lawful and right, he shall save his soul alive. "

APPENDIX.

NEWFOUNDLAND'S RESOURCES.

PROVIDENCE, R.I., U.S.A., Feb. 18, 1895.

SINCE I wrote the foregoing pages, some papers have come into my hands referring to Major-general Dashwood's attacks upon the credibility of those who are trying to make the resources of Newfoundland known in Great Britain.

Much depends on the point of view from which a man writes; and I can only say that, if the distinguished Major-general is right, *from a purely British point of view*, in depreciating the island and its resources, he thereby furnishes a *very strong argument why Great Britain should, for a reasonable compensation, cede this island to the United States.* I am perfectly sure that the majority of the 200,000 inhabitants would not have the slightest objection to exchange the Union Jack for the stars and stripes. But I do not think that, in making this exchange myself, I have abandoned my old English habits of thought; and so I would mention some reasons why, even if I were still a fellow-citizen (or should I say subject?) of Major-general Dashwood, and were as much bound as he is to place the interests of the British crown above every other interest of my life, I should for that very reason differ with him in opinion, first of all, from a strategic point of view. We must not, because my distinguished fellow-citizen, Captain Mahan, has so brilliantly painted the sea-power of England, forget also her *man-power*. Most certainly, Viscount Wolseley would not do so; and I think Major-general Dashwood, from whose interesting little book, "Chipplequorgan," I

have learned that he came with his regiment to Halifax
after the "Trent" affair, will agree with me that it would
then, in case of a war with the United States of America, have
been very convenient if Newfoundland had been peopled
by half a million hardy farmers, woodmen, and miners, in
addition to its few fisher-folk. England has to take under-
grown and underfed boys into her army now; but, if the
sturdy Irishmen who have been driven to the United States
by famine and eviction had been provided each with the
"three acres and a cow" of Joseph Chamberlain's speeches
in the valleys of the Humber or Codroy Rivers, surely the
experience of Louisbourg and a hundred well-fought battles
since then may tell us how much more they would have con-
tributed to Britain's honor and interest than they do now
as American voters. The south-western part of Newfoundland reminds one very much of old Ireland in its climate
and its physical features, and certainly is quite as well fitted
to sustain a sturdy peasantry of small land-owners.

The best answer to the distinguished officer's objections
may be found in the official reports of the geological survey
of Newfoundland, published by Edward Stanford, Charing
Cross, London. The present director of that survey, Mr.
James P. Howley, F.R.G.S., has replied in part to Major-
general Dashwood's remarks in a letter written a fortnight
ago, from which I extract a few passages. The Major-general said at the Royal Geographical Society that the timber
of Newfoundland is all scrub, and fit only for firing. Mr.
Howley writes: "Our lumbering industry is in a most flour-
ishing condition. Ten large saw-mills are in full swing,
besides several smaller ones, around our northern and
western bays. Large shipments of lumber were made last
summer to the English markets. Messrs. Watson & Todd,
of Liverpool, England, purchased 3,000,000 feet of lumber
in the island last summer; and the market quotations
in the Liverpool trade journals will be the best index to
the value of the lumber. The Exploits Milling Company

at Botwoodsville purchased $25,000 worth of stores in Montreal to be used in the winter's lumber-felling operations. They calculate on cutting 100,000 pine logs. Though the mill has been ten years in operation, the lumber shows no signs of exhaustion; while the other and far more abundant products of the Newfoundland forests, such as fir, spruce, birch, tamarack, etc., have scarcely been touched.

"The Benton Mill, owned by Messrs. Reid, contractors for the Northern & Western Railroad, though scarcely a year in existence, has put out 3,000,000 feet of first-class lumber."

As to the coal fields, Mr. Howley, referring to his own official reports for 1889, 1891, and 1892, as published by Stanford, writes : —

In the Bay St. George coal fields 16 distinct seams were discovered, ranging from a few inches up to several feet in thickness : the Cleary seam has 26 inches good coal ; Juke's seam, 4.6 feet ; Murray seam, 5.4 feet : Howley seam, 4.2 feet.

In the Grand Lake carboniferous area 15 distinct seams were discovered, also ranging from a few inches to several feet. Two seams on Coal Brook show 2.4 and 3.5 feet. On Aldery Brook, three seams show 2.6 feet, 3.8 feet, and 14 feet of coal. At Kelvin Brook 3 seams contain 2.6 feet, 3.8 feet, and 7 feet.

Specimens have been submitted to experts in connection with the Colonial Office, and have been found, in some cases, superior to the Cape Breton coal. So much for the report of a man who understands his business, and has had better opportunities than any other living man of studying the question.

For myself, I may say that during twenty years of travel, in which I have been from the Gulf of Mexico to Ottawa, and from the Straight Shore of Avalon to the Muir Glacier of Alaska, I have studied every State which I have visited with a view to its attractions for British emigrants, and, before the passing of our present absurd immigration laws, have been instrumental in transferring many skilled operatives from the foul slums of Manchester and Salford to the healthy and pleasant factory villages of New England.

I need hardly say that Newfoundland is not the right place for such men; but, under a just and wise imperial government, it can be made a happy home for thousands of hardy Scotch and Irish peasants, who need not, in crossing the ocean, change their political allegiance. But England must first do her duty.

She must build her railroad from Port aux Basques along the French shore to Bonne Bay, or further north, so as to give the people a means of communication which shall not be impeded by the French treaty rights; and she must arrange her tariffs so as to defend her fishermen against the unjust discrimination of foreign bounties. As an American, I can have no interest in saying these things to Englishmen. If Major-general Dashwood is right, so much the better for us.

Our Whitneys are awakening new life amid the ruins of Louisbourg, although the Duke of York and those who followed him as proprietors of the Sydney coal fields could do so little with them; and so, if England cannot help Newfoundland, *America can*, and can serve herself well at the same time. Take the fishing for an instance. The French bounties do not hurt the Massachusetts fishermen, because we have a *home* market which the Frenchmen cannot touch, and seek only a foreign market for the very small quantity that our own people do not consume. And to share in this American *home market* alone would be more profitable to Newfoundland than all its connection with England can ever be.

J. F.